Worry WARRIORS

Raintree is an imprint of Capstone Global Library Limited, a company incorporated in
England and Wales having its registered office at 264 Banbury Road, Oxford, OX2 7DY
– Registered company number: 6695582

www.raintree.co.uk
myorders@raintree.co.uk

Editor: Michelle Bisson
Designer: Hilary Wacholz

ISBN 978 1 4747 2845 4 (paperback)
20 19 18 17 16
10 9 8 7 6 5 4 3 2 1

British Library Cataloguing in Publication Data
A full catalogue record for this book is available from the British Library.

Every effort has been made to contact copyright holders of material reproduced in
this book. Any omissions will be rectified in subsequent printings if notice is given to
the publisher.

All the Internet addresses (URLs) given in this book were valid at the time of going
to press. However, due to the dynamic nature of the Internet, some addresses
may have changed, or sites may have changed or ceased to exist since publication.
While the author and publisher regret any inconvenience this may cause readers,
no responsibility for any such changes can be accepted by either the author or the
publisher.

Printed and bound in China.

Worry
WARRIORS

Jittery Jake
Conquers Stage Fright

by Marne Ventura
illustrated by Leo Trinidad

raintree

a Capstone company — publishers for children

CONTENTS

ALL ABOUT THE Worry WARRIORS

My name is Jake Williams. I live with my mother and sister in a city near the sea. My dad and mum split up before I was born, so it's always been just the three of us. I'm nine years old. Sometimes Mum calls me Little Neil. That's because I have curly black hair and dark brown skin like the famous astrophysicist Neil deGrasse Tyson. Also because I want to be a scientist some day. One great thing about my neighbourhood is that my three best friends live on my street. Adam, Nellie, Estella and I have known each other since pre-school.

Estella is an expert on movies and TV shows. She knows the names of all the actors, especially the kids. She loves dancing and cheerleading. She also likes hanging out with her family.

Nellie likes reading, writing, word games, and school. That's excellent because she wants to be a writer when she grows up.

Adam is awesome at sport, art, and building projects. He has dyslexia. That means he learns to read, write and spell differently from most kids.

WORRY WARRIORS UNITE

Three summers ago, when we were six, we were making hula-hoop bubbles in Nellie's back garden. We were barefoot, running around on the wet grass. Estella almost stepped on a bee. She freaked out. She ran into Nellie's house and wouldn't budge until Adam scooped up the bee with a plastic cup and put it into the bin.

Then Estella said she felt silly, being scared of teeny bees. But that she felt better after she told us and we didn't laugh at her.

I guess Nellie didn't want Estella to feel silly alone, because she told us that she was afraid of the dark at bedtime. She imagined scary stuff, like that her toys might come to life and attack her, or that monsters might be hiding in her wardrobe.

Then Adam said he gets scared walking across the bridge over the dual carriageway. He holds onto his mum's hand and doesn't look down.

So I told my friends my own babyish secret. I was afraid to wade into the sea because I could feel slimy stuff with my feet. What if I stepped on a poisonous jellyfish?

After we told each other our worries, we felt better. We didn't make fun of each other the way some kids would. And, if all of us had secret worries, maybe they weren't silly at all.

That's when Nellie had a great idea. She said we should form a club. First we would tell each other our worries. Then together we would fight them, like knights and warrior princesses in shining armour.

And that's how we became the Worry Warriors.

Chapter 1

Winter extravaganza

It's a Monday afternoon in late November. I'm sitting at a table outside the Sea View Primary School hall with Adam, Estella, and Nellie. We've just finished lunch. The Christmas holidays are three weeks away, but it's still warm and sunny. I watch a monarch butterfly glide across the courtyard. It drifts towards the eucalyptus trees at the edge of the playground.

"Dad said he'd walk with me to The Bookworm after school," says Nellie. "A new book in my mystery series is out. Do you guys want to come?"

"I would, but I've got football practice," says Adam. He swings his feet under the bench.

"Yes," says Estella. "No dance class today."

"Okay," I say. "I just have to do a couple of chores first. I'm trying to earn enough money to buy a robot racing car that I can control from my computer."

"Awesome," says Adam. "How do you control it?"

"You know that class mum signed me up for last summer at the University for Kids programme?" I say. "I learned to write computer programs that give directions. I can send the directions from the computer to the car, and it moves the way I tell it to!"

"How much is it?" asks Adam.

"£99.95," I reply. "I've just started saving. So far I have last week's pocket money, plus a bit extra: nine pounds total."

"Only £90.95 to go," Nellie says, smiling. "But don't forget postage and packing."

"I didn't think of that," I say. "Maybe more than £90.95 to go. If the VAT tax is 8 per cent, that will add eight pounds. And if shipping is 10 per cent, that's another ten pounds."

"You are good at maths!" Nellie says.

"I know," I say. "Two more weeks' pocket money." I wonder how I'm ever going to save that much but keep that worry to myself.

The end-of-lunch-break bell rings, and we head back to class. Estella, Adam, and I are in Ms Anderson's year 5 class. Nellie is next door in Mr Meaney's. Before school started, she was nervous about getting a new teacher and about being in a different class to us. But he's nice, despite his name, and we still get to spend some time together at school.

After we line up, Ms Anderson says, "We're going back to the hall with Mr Meaney's class. We'd like to talk to you about the year 5's part in the upcoming Winter Performance."

Estella twirls around with her arms up and curved, ballerina-style. "Yippee," she says. "I hope it's a play."

"Oh, no!" Adam says. "I thought we were having finish-your-work time. I was going to finish my reading comprehension questions so I won't have homework after football."

"Not fair," I say. "This is our ICT time."

Every year on the night before the Christmas holidays, the older children put on a show in the hall. Everyone's family comes, and each year goes onstage for 20 minutes. Last year we made snowflakes to decorate the backdrop. We wore scarves and mittens and sang songs about winter.

It wasn't too bad. I'd never want to be an actor or a singer, but since the whole class was doing the same thing, it was okay. Still, I wouldn't mind skipping it. Especially if it means we have to miss our ICT time because we have to practise.

When we get to the hall, we sit down at the lunch tables. There's a whiteboard on an easel at the front.

"Tell us what you know about Greek mythology," says Ms Anderson.

Nellie raises her hand. "The Greeks wrote stories to explain how Earth was created."

Mr Meaney writes it on the whiteboard.

"What else?" asks Ms Anderson. I raise my hand and

she calls on me.

"They thought the world was flat like a paper plate," I say, "and that Greece was in the centre. *So* not right." The kids laugh.

Brittany, the new girl in Nellie's class, raises her hand. "There were lots of gods and goddesses," she says. "Like Zeus and Athena."

Wow. Brittany is not just pretty. She's smart.

"Well done," says Ms Anderson. "Words and themes from Greek mythology are still used today. Have you heard of the Midas touch?"

"That means you're good at making money," says Nellie.

"Right," says Mr Meaney. "We're going to do a play about King Midas. He turned everything he touched into gold."

Ms Anderson asks Brittany to hand out a pile of booklets. "These folders contain the myth and the play. Your homework for tonight is to read them. Mr Meaney

and I have assigned your parts," Ms Anderson says. "You'll find them on the last page."

Brittany hands me a folder. I look at her as I take it. Her eyes are amazingly blue. I guess I should be paying closer attention to my hand than her eyes, though, because the folder slides out before I can grab it. It lands on Brittany's foot. "Sorry," I say, as I lean over to get it.

At the same time, Brittany bends down to pick up the folder and we bump heads.

"Sorry," we both say.

I want to ask her if she's okay, but she moves away.

That was stupid. My face feels hot.

I push my glasses up and open my folder. I wonder what job I've got? Usually I'm the one who turns the lights or the music on and off at the right time. I'd be okay with that.

But when I get to the cast and crew list, I can't believe what I see. Ms Anderson has given me the part of King Midas.

Chapter 2

Robot racing car

Nellie is waiting outside our classroom when Estella, Adam and I come out. We always walk home together.

"What part did you get?" she asks.

"King Midas!" I put on my rucksack. "Why would they choose *me* for the lead part?"

"You're smart," says Estella. "You have a good memory, and you are a great reader. I think it's great. I'm one of your three princess daughters. I'm so excited. I wonder what the costumes are like? I hope I get a long, sparkly dress."

"I hope I don't!" I blurt out. They all laugh and I blush.

"I know that didn't make sense," I say, "but I hate the idea of getting up on stage in front of people. I was hoping to help backstage. Do you think I'll have to wear a costume?"

"Definitely." Estella smiles, like that's a good thing. "Probably a cloak. And a crown, for sure."

"No way," I protest. "I'm not going onstage in front of everybody in a cloak."

"I'm head set designer." Adam kicks a rock across the pavement. "I get to make the stage look like a castle. How cool is that?"

"I'm narrator," Nellie says quietly. "Narrator is a big part."

"You'll be great," I say. "It's me I'm worried about."

No one knows what to say, but by now we're in front of Nellie's house, so we just say goodbye.

I go home, find my key, open the door and go inside. Mum teaches maths at Monarch Academy, so we usually get home at the same time. If Mum's not here, I'm supposed to call her mobile phone.

"Hi Jake!" she answers. "I've got held up at a meeting. I

should be home soon. Everything okay?"

"Yes," I say. "Can I go to The Bookworm with Nellie and Estella? Nellie's dad is going too."

"Okay," she says. "As long as you first check in on Mrs Jensen."

Mrs Jensen lives in the flats next to us. She was a teacher at Mum's school before she retired. She twisted her ankle last week, so she's hired me to help her with chores until her ankle heals.

I eat an apple, lock my front door, get Mrs Jensen's mail, and knock on her door.

She calls out, "Come on in, Jake."

Mrs Jensen's white Scottie dog runs up and wags his tail. His whole back end wiggles.

"Hi, Magnus," I say. I give him a scratch behind the ears.

Mrs Jensen's leg is propped up on a footrest. It's weird to see her sitting down. Usually she's riding her bike, jogging with Magnus, or working in the community garden.

"How's your ankle?" I ask as I hand her the post.

"Getting better." She wiggles her foot. "A few more days and I'll be back to normal."

"Good! Is it okay if Magnus walks with us to The Bookworm?" I ask. "Nellie's dad is going too."

"Of course, if you don't mind staying outside with him while the others go in."

"That's fine. Do you need anything else?" I ask.

"Will you drop the envelopes from the kitchen table into the postbox on your way?" she asks.

"No problem!" I reply, as I put Magnus on his lead.

Magnus and I jog to Nellie's. Estella, Nellie and Nellie's dad are waiting by the front door.

Nellie's dad is really cool. He's a computer programmer. It's fun to talk to him about technology. He really gets the stuff that interests me.

As we walk, I tell him about the robot racing car I'm saving up for.

"Sounds great," he says. "Can you control the speed as well as the direction?"

"Yes," I say. "It even has bluetooth, so you can run it wirelessly."

"Nice," says Nellie's dad. "Like a driverless car!"

"I've worked out it will take six more weeks to save enough," I say. "I get nine pounds pocket money, and I can earn an extra ten pounds from Mum and Mrs Jensen by walking Magnus and helping them both in the garden. But I can't spend money on anything else! It's going to be hard. Seven weeks is a long time."

"It'll go by fast," says Nellie's dad. "You know what they say – time flies when you're having fun!"

***

We get to The Bookworm, and I sit down on the bench outside to wait with Magnus. The bookshop owners must like dogs, because there's a water bowl by the door. Magnus laps up a drink. Then he sits and stares at me. His ears point up. The fur around his mouth is drippy. I think he's

smiling. I scratch his head and watch the people walk by. It's a good thing I'm staying outside. Whenever I go into The Bookworm, I find a book I want and buy it with my pocket money.

***

"I wanted a good part in the play," says Nellie as we walk home. She's got three new books tucked under one arm. "But now I feel super-nervous."

"I didn't even *want* a part," I tell her.

"It'll be fun." Estella twirls around a lamp-post. "Nellie, what costume do you think the narrator will wear?"

"Oh, no!" Nellie shrieks. "I hadn't thought of that. Will I have to look like a Greek statue or something?" Nellie shifts her books to the other arm.

"Brittany and Ashley play my sisters," says Estella. "I wonder if we'll have matching gowns. And crowns?"

"Brittany's a princess?" I ask. This play is making me so anxious.

"The way I learned it, King Midas only had one daughter," says Nellie's dad.

"They added two for the play," says Nellie. "So more kids could have speaking parts."

"Makes sense. Too bad you can't build a robot to do your part, Jake," Nellie's dad says, winking at me. "Then you could control it from behind the scenes."

"I wish!" I say. His idea makes me smile, but also makes me more nervous. It also makes me wonder if I could build my own robot racing car for less money than the one I'm saving up for. But, I don't think I'm that good at electronics yet.

"We sing a song at the end," says Estella. "It's going to be so fun."

"Wait?! Who sings? " I ask. "Everyone sings? I am *not* singing by myself."

All this talk about the play gives me the jitters. I'd better get home and read it. I say goodbye, and Magnus and I jog back to Mrs Jensen's.

"Thanks, Jake," she says when I return Magnus. "I don't know what I'd do without you."

She hands me a five pound note.

"You don't need to pay me," I tell her. Mrs Jensen is almost like a grandmother. I've known her ever since I can remember.

"I know," she says. "But I want to. And I'm sure you're saving up for something."

I tell her about my racing car and she agrees that it sounds fantastic.

£85.95 to go! It's going to be a long time before I get that car. Or have any spending money for other stuff. If Nellie's dad is right, and time flies when you're having fun, I guess I'm going to have to figure out how to have a lot of fun for free.

Chapter 3

King Midas

When I get home I hear Mum in the kitchen. "Yum!" I call, when I get a whiff of chilli and rice. "I'm home!"

I go to my room and add my earnings to my money jar. I find a marker and write RACING CAR on both sides, to remind me not to spend any on other stuff. Then I grab my folder and take it out to the kitchen.

"How's it going, Jake?" Mum gives me a hug. "Do you have homework?"

"I have to read this play," I say. "Can you believe Ms Anderson made me King Midas for the Winter Extravaganza?"

"Why, Jake, that's wonderful!" Mum gives me a kiss on the head.

"Wonderful? It's horrible." I open the folder and start to read. "Oh, no," I say, when I reach the end. "It's worse than I imagined. Look at all these lines I have to memorize."

I hand Mum the folder.

"And I think I have to wear a costume. I don't even like wearing costumes for Halloween."

"This is the lead part," says Mum as she reads. "Ms Anderson clearly thinks you can do it."

"Maybe. But it means I'll miss ICT time," I say. "And I wanted to earn extra money after school to buy a robot racing car, not spend my time memorizing lines. It'll take forever!"

"You'll be great," Mum says. "Besides, myths are interesting. Ancient people who created myths were like Worry Warriors, in a way."

"What do you mean?"

"People can be frightened of things they don't understand," she explains. "Before science, they made up stories to explain nature. Like, why there's lightning."

"What does the myth of King Midas explain?" I ask.

"It's a different kind of myth," says Mum. "It explains human nature."

I'm about to ask Mum what that means when Amanda comes into the kitchen with her homework.

Amanda and Nellie's big sister, Lucy, are cheerleaders at Monarch Academy. They must have been practising today, because Amanda's wearing her blue and grey uniform, and a blue and grey bow in her curly ponytail. People say that Amanda looks like a mini-Mum. I'm not so sure. After all, mum wears glasses, like me. Amanda can see perfectly without them.

Amanda sits down next to me at the kitchen table and sees my folder.

"Year 5 Greek mythology play?" she asks.

I nod. "I have to be King Midas! I don't want to do it."

"We did Pandora's Box when I was in year 5. I wanted to be Pandora, but I had to turn the lights and music on and off backstage," she says sadly.

"That's what I wanted to do! Life is so unfair!" I say.

Amanda nods. "You can say that again."

"Why is life unfair for you?" I ask.

"Too much homework!," she exclaims. "Wait until you get to secondary school, Jake. Instead of one teacher giving you one piece of homework, you'll have six teachers giving it to you. Tonight I have maths, English, and geography."

"Want to help me practise my lines when you've finished?" I ask Amanda. "And then play a video game?"

"By the time I finish, it'll be bedtime," she says.

"That's rubbish," I say, but what I'm thinking again is: life is so unfair.

"Amanda," says Mum, "your turn to set the table."

Amanda heaves a sigh, then puts her homework aside and sets the table as Mum dishes up the food.

As we eat, I say, "Mum, do you think I could ask Ms Anderson to give me a different job in the play? Like a backstage job?"

"I know you didn't choose to be King Midas," says Mum, "but it's an honour to be given the lead part. And doing things that are unfamiliar and challenging can be good for you."

Great. Just what I didn't want to hear. Mum is usually right, but … it still scares me.

"What were the costumes like when your class did the Greek mythology play?" I ask Amanda.

"Togas," she says. "And a crown of leaves. I was sad I didn't get to wear one."

"I don't want to wear a toga," I say. "What *is* a toga?"

"You know, those loose white dresses the Greeks wore," says Amanda. "With a gold belt, and sandals."

I eat a spoonful of chilli and imagine being onstage in a dress.

"I feel sick," I say.

Mum puts her hand on my forehead.

"Not that kind of sick," I tell her, though I do kind of

feel like I want to throw up. "Sick, like, I don't want to be in the play."

"You should be happy," says Amanda. "You have the best part!"

"But what if I forget my lines?" I say. "What if I look silly in a toga? What if the other kids laugh at me?"

"I know just what you need," Amanda says, smiling at Mum.

Mum nods, puts one arm around my shoulder, and holds out the phone to Amanda with the other. "Let's give the phone to King Midas. He needs to set up an emergency Worry Warriors meeting."

Chapter 4

Emergency meeting

The next day after school, Nellie, Adam, Estella and I meet in Nellie's tree house in her back garden. That's where we always have our Worry Warriors meetings.

The tree house is really cool. Nellie's dad built it for Nellie's big brother, Henry, when he was little. Henry started secondary school this year, and he's on the athletics team, so he's pretty busy. He lets us use it whenever we want.

We put on the Viking helmets that we got at the after-Halloween sale a couple of years ago. We know we're a bit old for this now, but it's tradition!

Then we raise our hands and yell, "Don't worry, be happy!" That's our Worry Warriors battle cry. It's how we always start meetings.

"I hereby call this meeting to order," says Nellie. "Let's start by saying what worries us about being in the school play."

We all settle into beanbag chairs.

"And remember," says Estella, "Nobody is allowed to say someone's worry is stupid."

"Right," says Adam. "What happens in the tree house, stays in the tree house."

"No making fun or laughing," I add.

"I'm excited about being narrator," says Nellie. "But I read the script last night, and I can't believe how many lines I have."

"Me too," I say. "And we can't read them. We have to know them by heart."

"That's show business," says Estella. "You have to memorize your lines."

"But you only have a few," I tell her. "Nellie and I have so many."

"I'm really glad I get to paint the set," says Adam.

Estella flips through her folder. "You're right," she says. "Why don't I have more lines?"

"What happens if we forget our lines?" asks Nellie.

"Does Ms Anderson think I can't handle a bigger part?" asks Estella.

"Will we get to use cue cards?" I ask. "I hope so."

"Ms Anderson gave us directions for a toga costume," I tell Nellie. "Did Mr Meaney give you the same thing?"

Nellie nods.

"It looks easy. They're going to give us the fabric," says Estella. "We just have to tie it on and pin it up the sides. And make a belt, and wear sandals."

"But it'll look stupid," I say. "It only goes over one shoulder. I don't want to wear a dress."

"You three seem to be getting more nervous," says Adam. "Maybe it's time for us to make a plan for fighting our worries. What can we do?"

"Go on strike?" I say.

"Leave a week early for the Christmas holidays?" says Nellie. "We'll say we're visiting our grandparents."

"Be serious,"" says Estella. "Let's figure out how to do a good job. I want to show Ms Anderson I'm ready for a bigger part in the next play."

"If we practise every day we can learn our lines," says Nellie. "We have to work at it."

"What about earning money for my racing car?" I say. "And other homework? When am I going to find the time to learn lines?"

"We can practise when we're walking to school, and when we're in the playground," says Nellie. "That way you'll have time for other stuff after school."

"Good idea," says Estella.

"I'm going to ask about cue cards," I say.

Adam says, "Ms Anderson taught me how to make this cool tick chart. It helps me keep track of all the things I have to do. We can make one for you, Jake."

"I'll walk Magnus if you run out of time," says Estella.

"Wow, thanks, you guys," I say.

"I sort of feel better," says Nellie.

"I guess if I'm stuck being King Midas, I'd rather do a good job than mess it up." I say.

There's a knock on the tree house door, and Lucy sticks her head in. "Want to come and try a cupcake?"

"Meeting adjourned," Adam says.

We raise our arms and chant, "Don't worry, be happy!" before we head to the kitchen.

Adam's eyes get big when he sees the cupcakes on the kitchen table. "How many did you make?"

"We need three dozen for the fundraiser," says Amanda. "But we have extras." She hands one to Adam.

"Butterfly cupcakes," says Estella. "That's so cool. I want to be a cheerleader and bake cupcakes like this when I'm in year 7."

"Here, Nellie," Amanda says. She hands her a cupcake.

There's a butterfly on top of the chocolate icing. The wings are made from mini-pretzels, and the head is an orange M&M.

"They're so cute!" says Nellie.

"They taste good, too," says Adam, with a mouthful of cake.

I almost don't want to bite into my cupcake because it looks so cool. Amanda and I used to have fun baking stuff together. She's a genius at coming up with creative decorations. Sometimes it seems like Amanda's good at everything. It was fun having her for a big sister when we both went to the same school. I miss that.

"I hope we sell all of our cupcakes," says Lucy. "We're trying to raise enough for cheerleader week away."

"Speaking of money, I've got to go and see if Mrs Jensen needs help," I say. "And walk Magnus. See you guys later."

As I jog to Mrs Jensen's, I think about the Worry Warriors meeting. I feel less nervous about playing King Midas. But I really have a lot of work to do.

Chapter 5

First rehearsal

Our street has a community garden where both Mum and Mrs Jensen grow vegetables. Mum pays me my pocket money for doing chores at home. If I help her in the garden, I get extra. And Mrs Jensen needs me to tend her garden until her ankle heals. She pays me too.

So, for the rest of the week, I'm pretty busy after school. First I check with Mrs Jensen to see if she needs any errands running. Then I walk around the block a few times with Magnus.

Magnus is really smart. He knows to stop and wait at the crossing if there are cars going by. He's good on his lead unless he sees a squirrel. Then he goes crazy trying to chase it. He likes to dig holes, so if I take him with me when I work in the garden, I have to keep an eye on him. No one ever said walking a dog was easy.

Working in the garden is fun. Mum shows me how to pick the pumpkins, courgettes and tomatoes. Then we plant seeds for carrots, lettuce, spinach, beetroot and broccoli. I tell her about my robot racing car, and she helps me practise my lines. Magnus follows me around and watches me work.

By Thursday I have nineteen pounds in my racing car jar.

I don't know my lines by heart yet, but Ms Anderson says we can read from our scripts at the first rehearsal tomorrow.

After dinner I take a break and practise my computer programming. I can't wait to get that racing car robot and make it go.

It's not bedtime yet, so I ask Amanda to play a video game with me.

"Can't," she says. "More homework."

I try a few rounds of the video game by myself. But, it's

not that much fun to play alone.

Then it's time for bed. I try to think about video games and racing cars as I fall asleep, and *not* think about tomorrow's rehearsal.

The next day after lunch all the year 5s go to the hall.

"Wow," I tell Adam, when I see the backdrop. "How did you make it look like stones?"

"I used a big sponge, and dipped it into paint," says Adam. "And stamped it here and there. Pretty cool, isn't it?"

"Super-cool," I say.

"Nice," says Nellie.

"Like a real castle," says Estella.

"Let's start at the beginning," says Ms Anderson.

We're sitting at lunch tables. Mr Meaney stands behind us.

"Everyone who's in the first act, come up," says Ms Anderson.

Nellie, Estella and I climb the steps on one side

of the stage. "Look," says Estella as we're going up. She points to a big box of white cloth on the floor in front of the stage. It's labelled COSTUMES. "I hope we're getting our toga fabric today."

Brittany and Ashley come up, along with 10 other kids who are servants and royal advisors.

"Go ahead, Nellie," says Mr Meaney. "Read from the script if you don't know your lines yet."

Nellie opens her folder and begins. "Many years ago, in ancient Greece, there lived a king who loved gold."

This is where I'm supposed to walk out to my royal counting house. Right now it's just a lunch table that Adam and some other kids have set up. There's a box on top, full of fake gold.

I walk out, open my folder, and read my first lines. "Gold, gold, gold! How I love gold."

"A little louder, Jake," says Ms Anderson. She's standing at the front of the stage. She wears dangly earrings that match the seasons. Today they're snowflakes.

They swing as she walks across to the other side. "I'm sure you can remember that line now," she says. "Say it again. Look up at the audience and project your voice."

I look up and see Mr Meaney and the other year 5s watching me. Mr Meaney holds up a hand and says, "I need to hear you from out here. Don't look at the microphone, but talk towards it."

Reading from my folder isn't so bad. But looking up and saying stuff to a load of people in the hall is nerve-wracking. Where is the mic?

"Go ahead," says Ms Anderson.

I spot the mic and move towards it. "I do love gold. Gold, gold, gold." The mic makes a loud, cracking sound. Everyone laughs. My face feels hot.

"Good try, Jake!" Adam calls to me from the side of the stage.

"Better," says Mr Meaney. "Don't worry about the mic. We'll get it adjusted."

They're all being nice but it's just making me nervous.

"Not quite so close to the mic this time, Jake. Pick up a handful of gold coins as you talk," says Ms Anderson. "Show us you love gold."

"One more time," Ms Anderson smiles at me.

My hands are sweaty. I forget my line and have to look at my folder.

I dig one hand into the box and scoop up some coins. "Gold, gold, gold. How I love gold." When I turn towards the mic, half of the coins fall out of my hand and onto the stage. One rolls on its edge to the front of the stage, spins around, and drops off. Everyone laughs.

"Let's move on," says Ms Anderson. "Where are the princesses?"

Estella, Brittany, and Ashley come onstage as I pick up the gold.

"Go ahead, girls," says Ms Anderson.

Brittany and Ashley open their folders.

Estella knows her line. She smiles and steps towards me. "Father, it is time for our royal breakfast."

"Perfect," says Mr Meaney. "Good projecting, Estella."

Estella smiles and curtsies. The kids clap.

Brittany and Ashley step up, next to Estella.

"It's okay to read," says Ms Anderson.

Ashley reads, "The royal cook is bringing golden apples, golden eggs, and golden raisin bread."

"Aren't you tired of gold food, Father?" I read. I hold my head up and try to project my voice.

The kids laugh.

"That's okay, Jake. You read Brittany's line. You'll get it." Ms Anderson gives me a thumbs-up.

This is hard. It's hot with the stage lights on. I hope we've almost finished. I wish I were in ICT right now.

"Step towards the front of the stage while Brittany speaks," says Ms Anderson. "You don't want to stand in front of her. Make sure the audience can see and hear her."

Brittany and I are facing each other, with our sides to the audience. I step sideways towards the front of the stage. I'm looking at Brittany to see if I'm blocking her.

Brittany looks up from her folder and smiles at me. I hope I don't look as sweaty as I feel. I push my glasses up on my nose. Just to make sure I'm not blocking her, I take one more sideways step.

That's when I fall off the stage and land right in the middle of the costume box.

Chapter 6

Human nature

"That could have happened to anybody," says Adam as we walk home.

"It wasn't that bad," says Estella.

"It was a graceful fall," says Nellie.

"I don't want to talk about it," I say.

Nellie insists. "We need another Worry Warrior's meeting. I'm nervous but I think you're even more jittery, Jake."

"Can we please stop talking about it? I just want to go home, walk Magnus, and play around on my computer."

"Nellie's right," says Estella. "You'll feel better if you talk about it."

"After the meeting, we can kick the football around," says Adam. "That always makes me feel better."

"You know what?" says Nellie. "We can have meetings every day after school. We'll practise our lines so much that it will be impossible for us to mess up."

"Really?" I say. "What about Magnus and Mrs Jensen? And homework?"

"And football?" asks Adam.

"And ballet?" asks Estella.

"Just for half an hour," says Nellie. "Come straight home from school with me. You'll still be finished in time for your other stuff."

"I guess that would be okay," I say. "Now that we've had our first rehearsal, I can see I need a lot of practice."

"Tomorrow's Saturday," Nellie says. "Can you guys do a kick-off meeting in the morning?"

We all agree to meet at Nellie's the next day.

Mrs Jensen lets me take Magnus to Nellie's house for

our meeting. He lies on a beanbag chair with his head on his paws and watches us. When we raise our hands and say "Don't worry, be happy!" his tail wags.

Nellie starts. "I didn't know it was going to be so scary up on stage."

"I know," I say. "Remember last year's show? The hall looked so big and far away. It was super-hot onstage. And with the lights in my eyes, it was hard to see the audience. I felt like a million strangers were staring at me. But at least last year, they were staring at *all* of us. Not just at me."

"When we had our dance recital last month, I wasn't nervous at practice," says Estella. "But on the night of the performance, I was scared. I told my mum I'd changed my mind and didn't want to do it."

"What happened?" asks Adam.

"My teacher showed me how to breathe," Estella puts her hand on her stomach and sucks in air. "And then relax my muscles like cooked noodles." She slumps over like a rag doll.

It looks pretty silly. "That helps?" I ask.

"It does," says Estella. "Also, she told me to focus on doing a good job, not on the audience. She said to pretend I'm doing a perfect rehearsal."

Adam says, "When I had to give that speech in class last year, I was scared. You guys know I have trouble reading out loud. I memorized the speech by listening to a recording, and then when I practised giving the speech, my mum made a video of me."

"Did that help?" I ask.

"Yes, it helped a lot," says Adam. "Want to try it? Since I don't have lines to learn, I could be the cameraman for you guys. I can use my tablet."

"Okay," says Nellie. "Let's read through our lines now. Monday we can try out our new ideas."

Adam and Magnus watch while we read our parts.

"You're good readers," says Adam. "But you look at your folders a lot."

"We need to learn our lines," says Nellie.

"I wonder if Ms Anderson would let me tape X's on the stage to show you where to stand, Jake?" asks Adam.

"Great idea!" I say.

Estella says, "Jake and I need to get into character. We need to *be* Princess Marigold and King Midas."

"How do we do that?" I ask.

"Pretend you're King Midas. *Be* King Midas."

I put my finger on Adam's arm. "You're gold," I say. "Hey, now I can trade you in for cash and get my remote-control racing car."

"Huh?" says Adam.

"Didn't you read the myth?" asks Nellie.

"I'm not in the play," he says.

"You're still supposed to read it," says Estella.

"I am?" Adam's pocket timer dings. "Saved by the bell," he laughs. "Football practice."

We adjourn the meeting and Magnus and I walk Adam to practice.

"Want to hear the story of King Midas?" I ask.

"Sure," says Adam.

"So, there's this king," I begin. "He loves gold more than anything. One day he finds a satyr – that's someone who is half goat, half man – in his rose garden. Midas is nice to the satyr, who turns out to be a friend of the god Dionysius. Dionysius wants to thank Midas for being kind to his friend. He gives him one wish."

"Cool," says Adam.

"King Midas's wish is to turn everything he touches into gold," I say. "But now he can't eat, because his food turns to gold. Worst of all, he accidentally turns his daughters to gold."

"Wow," says Adam.

"King Midas realizes he made a big mistake. He can't eat. He misses his daughters. He begs Dionysius to take away the wish."

"He should have said that wish differently," says Adam. "He should have just asked for a giant crate of gold."

"Yeah," I say. "But I think the point is more about human nature. King Midas was greedy. When he got his wish, he learned that his daughters were more important to him than gold."

"I guess," says Adam. "Still, we should think about what to wish for if we ever get the chance. So we don't mess it up like he did."

I think about the £19 in my money jar. Today is allowance day, so when I add nine pounds I'll have £28. It's going to take another five weeks to earn enough for a robot racing car. I wish Dionysius would give me a wish. Five minutes of Midas touch would come in handy right now.

Chapter 7

Beach Street Hobbies

I wake up on Sunday morning to the smell of bacon. That means Mum is making eggs and pancakes too. I grab my King Midas folder and go into the kitchen.

Mum is scrambling eggs. Six blueberry pancakes are in the pan, ready to be flipped.

Amanda is sitting at the kitchen table looking at cupcake-making ideas on the laptop.

"Want to help me practise my lines?" I ask her.

"No," she snaps, without looking up.

"You don't have to be rude," I snap back. Last year, Amanda helped me practise my songs a lot. Why is she so grumpy now?

I plop down, open my folder, and read my first lines. Then I try to say them without looking.

"How I love gold. Gold, gold, gold." After that, I'm stuck.

"Can you do that somewhere else?" asks Amanda. "I'm trying to concentrate."

"On cupcake decorations?" I say. "Who cares what a cupcake looks like if it tastes good?"

"Lots of people!" says Amanda. "What are you talking about? What's wrong with you?"

I know it was a mean thing to say, but Amanda started it. I blurt out, "You're always complaining that you have too much homework to help me with my lines or play video games like we used to, but you have plenty of time to decorate stupid cupcakes!"

"For your information," says Amanda, "Lucy and I are going to start a cupcake business. Cupcakes are just as important as your stupid robot racing car! Cupcakes are an art form. They make people happy!"

"Hey," says Mum as she puts butter, syrup, and orange juice on the table. "What's going on with you two? It's not like you to argue."

"Ask Amanda," I say. "She started it."

"Did not," says Amanda.

"Who started it doesn't matter. Stop it now," says Mum.

Amanda and I frown at each other as we eat.

"How's it going with the play?" Mum asks.

I'm glad for a change of subject. "If I had my lines on cards," I say, "it would make it easier to carry them around and practise."

"Why not type them into the computer after breakfast?" suggests Mum. "We can print them onto cards."

"Good idea!" I say.

Once the dishes are done I get to work. There are a lot of lines, but we learned typing in ICT in years 3 and 4, so I'm pretty fast. I find that typing the words helps me learn them.

Mum has card for the printer. She helps me format my document so we can print it out and trim it to index-card size with her paper cutter.

Then I have the idea of punching a hole in the corner of each card to hold them together with a ring. But we don't have any rings.

Mum says, "Let's walk into town and get some at Beach Street Hobbies. They have stationery stuff."

"I need a notebook for English, too," Amanda says to Mum. She isn't looking at me.

We put on our shoes and coats and head into town.

Beach Street is a busy place on a Sunday morning. People are sitting in cafés drinking coffee and reading newspapers. Dog walkers are crossing at the lights to go to the big park in the centre of town. Mums and dads are pushing babies in pushchairs.

"What do you want for your birthday dinner next weekend?" Mum asks Amanda. "Should we invite Lucy?"

"Yes," Amanda says. "I'd love that."

I forgot it was almost Amanda's birthday. Mum lets us choose our birthday dinner every year.

"Let's have spaghetti and salad," says Amanda. "And lemon blueberry cupcakes."

"Yum!" Mum says.

I don't say anything. If Amanda's still mad at me then I'm still mad at her.

***

Beach Street Hobbies is stocked for Christmas. The shop is huge, and the front aisles are covered with decorations. It smells like cinnamon and cloves. We walk past the ornaments, jingle bells and snowmen. Then we go past aisles of colourful wool and knitting needles. When we reach the school stationery, Amanda picks a notebook. I find four metal rings for my cards.

"Oh, look, Mum!" Amanda points to the next section. It's filled with cake-decorating equipment. There are brightly coloured cupcake cases, muffin tins, mixers, icing kits and cookbooks.

"When Lucy and I start our cupcake business, we're going to get all of this stuff."

The next aisle is covered with fake flowers and leaves. I think of my costume. "Mum, Ms Anderson gave me the cloth for my toga. But I need to make a leaf crown."

"Those are called laurel wreaths," says Mum. "We'll need a headband and some of these leaves."

"Also, I'm supposed to have a gold belt and sandals," I add.

"Let's get gold ribbon while we're here," says Mum. "We'll use some for a belt, and glue some to your flip-flops."

After we find everything, Mum pays for our stuff and we leave.

"I wish I didn't have to wear this costume," I tell Mum, as we walk back down Beach Street.

"What bothers you about it?" asks Mum.

"It's weird that it only goes over one shoulder," I say. "What if other kids laugh at me for wearing a dress?"

"They'll be wearing dresses, too, if they're in the play," says Mum.

"Good point," I say. "But what if it slips off? It's only tied at one shoulder."

"You can practise tying it tightly," says Mum. "I'll help you. Maybe I can sew in a snap or some Velcro."

"Can I wear jeans and a T-shirt underneath?" I ask.

"Amanda," says Mum, "do you remember how they did it when you were in year 5?"

I wonder if Amanda's going to answer. She still seems mad. But then she says, "No T-shirt. But the guys wore gym shorts underneath."

"Oh. Okay," I say. This is good information. At least if it slips off or falls apart, I won't be standing in the middle of the stage in my underwear. Of course, standing in the middle of the stage in nothing but my gym shorts doesn't sound that great, either.

Chapter 8

Dress rehearsal

The next week we practise every day after school in the Worry Warrior's tree house. Adam uses the video camera in his tablet to record us. It helps a lot. When I watch a recording of myself, I notice things. Like, that I'm not looking up. Or that I sound like I'm reading. We talk about it. Then we practise again and make it better.

By Thursday I can say most of my lines by heart. Estella says I sound more like King Midas and less like Jake.

Mum likes to sing, so while we make dinner or work in the garden, she helps me practise the song at the end of the play. It's called "The Best Things in Life Are Free." The good news is, everybody has to sing, not just King Midas.

I now have £43 in my jar. All that dog walking and vegetable gardening is fun, but it still feels like it's taking a long time to earn enough money for my robot racing car.

I'm glad Mrs Jensen's ankle is getting better. I can tell she doesn't like sitting around. I think she's almost as excited about the racing car as I am. I take our laptop over and show her how I can write programs to control the car. With my pocket money and the extra money, I should have enough in four more weeks. I practise my programming whenever I can, so I'll be ready.

Friday after lunch is the dress rehearsal. Ms Anderson says, "One more week until the Winter Extravaganza. Today you're going to wear your costumes and do the play as if it's the night of the performance. No stopping, or talking, or asking for help. Are we ready?"

Some children mumble and groan. Nellie, Estella, Adam and I look at each other and do a thumbs-up.

"I feel good about this," Nellie says when we're standing with Estella offstage.

We tie our toga fabric over our school clothes. It looks silly, if you ask me. And it keeps opening up on the sides. My costume definitely needs more work before next Friday.

Brittany, Ashley and the other children are on the opposite side of the stage.

Adam is over there, too. He's standing next to Ms Anderson. She signals Nellie to get ready. The royal advisors and servants find their places.

When everyone is settled, Nellie walks out in front of the closed curtain. I hear her say her line perfectly. "Many years ago, in ancient Greece, there lived a king who loved gold."

Then Adam pulls the cord to open the curtain.

I walk out to the middle of the stage and stand next to the table. "Gold, gold, gold. How I love gold," I say. So far, so good. The mic doesn't boom or crackle, and I remember my line. I look out at the audience. I even scoop up a few coins without dropping them.

The princesses come out and say their lines. Brittany

has a pretty gold clasp holding her toga at the shoulder. She looks like a real Greek princess. I feel myself starting to blush. I think of robots to calm down.

The play continues. The stage lights feel hotter and hotter. Wearing my toga over my school clothes does not help.

Still, things go well. I remember my lines while I am at breakfast with my princess daughters.

We go offstage, the curtain closes, and Adam and his team change the backdrop. Now we're in the castle rose garden.

I go out, find the satyr, and invite him to stay at the castle. Dionysius shows up and grants my wish.

One more change of backdrops and I'm back inside the castle. I realize I can't eat anything. My food turns to gold when I touch it. Then comes the big scene, where I turn my daughters to gold.

Estella, Brittany and Ashley skip across the stage, do a ballet twirl, and hold out their hands to me.

"Hello, Father," they say.

I touch their hands and they freeze. It's pretty awesome. They honestly look like statues.

"Oh, my daughters!" I say. "What have I done?"

I touch Estella, Ashley and Brittany on the head.

"I've turned my daughters to gold. Oh no!" I cry out.

Estella and Ashley are staring straight ahead, not moving a muscle. But Brittany moves her eyes and looks at me. I push my glasses up on the bridge of my nose. Why is it so hot up here? Now I've forgotten my next line.

I look to the side of the stage for Ms Anderson's cue card. Where is she? I take a small step and twist around to look at the other side. Oops, I bump into a chair and lose my balance.

I grab the first thing I can – the curtain. At first it feels solid and I tighten my grip on the velvet fabric. Then I hear a ripping sound. I feel myself falling. The harder I grip, the more ripping I hear. As the ripping stops, my feet slip out from under me and I land on my back on the hard wood

stage. The curtain must have ripped completely, because it lands on top of me. I'm lying on my back on the floor of the stage, covered by the ripped curtain.

I hear the kids in the hall laughing. I hear the children onstage laughing. I can't hear them, but I wouldn't be surprised if Ms Anderson and Mr Meaney were laughing, too.

I imagine what I look like: a big lump of ripped, red velvet. I'm not hurt, but I feel bad. I think I'll just stay under this curtain and never come out.

Chapter 9

Time flies when you're having fun

On Saturday morning Mum is busy in the kitchen when I get up.

"Hi Jake!" she says, cheerfully. She's pulling flour and sugar from the cupboard.

I pour myself a bowl of cereal. "What are you making?" I ask.

"Amanda's cupcakes," she replies. "Want to help?"

"Of course! Where's Amanda?" I pour milk and grab a spoon.

"She had to leave early for a cheerleader fundraising carwash," Mum says.

"Is Lucy coming tonight?" I ask.

"Yes," Mum answers. "I invited the whole family. Want to help me make a big pot of bolognaise?"

"Yeah." Mum, Amanda, and I have always had fun cooking together. There's a TV cooking show we like. This crazy man tells the science and history behind the food he cooks. Sometimes we try his recipes.

Now I pull up his website and get the recipe for bolognaise sauce. Mum and I read it together.

"We'll need to go to the supermarket," says Mum. "And I need decorations at Beach Street Hobbies."

I go to my room to put my shoes on, and think about what to give Amanda. When we were little, we made each other cards. Last year she was into this series of books about cheerleaders, and I got her the latest book. This year she wants a mobile phone, but that's too expensive. She likes new clothes, but I don't know how to pick those. I guess I'll take my money and look around at Beach Street Hobbies.

Mum drives us to the supermarket and we get what

we need. Then we go to Beach Street Hobbies and Mum chooses some decorations.

I see the cupcake-making stuff and remember how much Amanda liked it when we were there before. There's a set of icing tips that make different shapes. They're stainless steel. There are 25 different tips. They screw onto an icing bag that you fill with icing. It's like the one they use on Amanda's favourite TV cupcake show.

The kit is £39.95. That's a lot. If I get it, I'll have to wait another few weeks for my racing car. And that's if Mrs Jensen still needs me to work for her.

I'm trying to decide what to do when Mum comes down the aisle. "Find something?" she asks.

"I think Amanda would like this," I say.

"That's really nice," says Mum.

"It's a lot of money," I say. "But I have that much saved up so I can afford it."

"It is a lot to spend," says Mum. "Amanda would really like it. But you've been working hard to earn money for your racing car, too. Are you really ok with spending it all?"

"What do you think I should do?" I ask.

"You have to be the one to decide," says Mum. "We can look around for a bit longer if you'd like."

Even though I'm still sort of mad at her, I think Amanda is an amazing sister. If she wants to start a cupcake business with Lucy, I want her to have the right tools.

"I'm going to get it," I say.

"Are you sure?" asks Mum.

"I'm sure," I say.

By the time we get home, Mum and I are starving. We eat leftover pizza for lunch and then get to work on the bolognaise sauce.

Next, Mum helps me wrap my present, and then I go to check on Mrs Jensen and Magnus.

"Jake, I'm glad to see you," says Mrs Jensen. She's got her foot propped up again. "I think I overdid it yesterday.

I was hoping you could walk Magnus today."

"No problem," I tell Mrs Jensen. "I'm sorry you're still having trouble with your ankle."

"Thanks, Jake. I'll survive! More importantly, how's the play going?" she asks as I snap on Magnus's lead.

I tell her about the big disaster yesterday.

"That's what dress rehearsals are for," she says. "You make your mistakes then, so it will go smoothly at the real performance."

"I never thought of it that way," I say. I feel better. Maybe I've already made all of the mistakes there are to make. That would be awesome.

Amanda is home when I get back. She and Mum are decorating the cupcakes.

"Do you want help practising your lines when we've finished here?" asks Mum.

"I know my lines, but I'm worried about my toga," I tell her.

Amanda surprises me by saying, "I'll help you fix it so it won't fall off."

"Really?" I say.

"Of course," she says, as if we'd never had a fight.

I bring my costume out and tie the cloth on over my gym shorts. Amanda fixes the knot on one shoulder so it's tight. Then she uses safety pins to close the open sides. Now it feels really solid. I'm not worried about it falling off.

"What do you think?" I ask her.

"Looks like a dress," she says.

We both laugh.

"Hey, Amanda," I say. "I'm sorry I said your cupcakes are stupid."

"Yeah," she says. "I'm sorry I'm always so busy."

"I guess that's how it is when you get to secondary school," I say.

"Well," says Amanda. "You'll have an easier time of it when you get to year 7. You're good at school."

"Really?" I say. "It seems like you're good at everything."

"Schoolwork is harder for me," she says. "Especially maths."

"I'm sorry you didn't get to be the lead in your Greek play. You would have been way better at it than me," I say.

Amanda smiles and bumps my arm with her elbow. "You'll be great," she says.

I elbow-bump her back. It helps that my sister thinks I'll do well.

Next, we glue the leaves to the headband to make a laurel wreath. We glue gold ribbon onto my flip-flops, and add gold strings that go over my ankles in a criss-cross.

"Excellent," says Amanda when I have my entire costume on. "How does it feel?"

"Embarrassing," I say, as I unplug the glue gun. "But I don't think it'll fall off. Thanks again for your help!"

I feel better about my costume. But I'm glad it's time to take it off and get ready for Amanda's birthday dinner.

I blow up balloons and hang the Happy Birthday banner while Amanda sets the table and Mum makes a salad. The doorbell rings, and Nellie's family is here.

I show Nellie's dad and big brother, Henry, the website for my robot car. They agree, it's going to be awesome!

"This spaghetti bolognaise is good!" says Lucy to Mum after we all sit down and start dinner.

"Jake helped," says Mum.

Lucy gives me a thumbs-up.

Henry eats two big helpings, so I know he likes it.

Then it's time for dessert. Mum arranges 12 cupcakes on a fancy plate. Each one has a candle in the middle. She lights them and we sing "Happy Birthday" to Amanda. She takes a deep breath and blows them out.

Next, it's time to open presents. Amanda unwraps mine last. Her eyes open wide when she sees the decorating kit.

"You got that for me, Jake?" she says. "Lucy, look at all these tips!

"It's amazing!" Lucy smiles.

"Thank you, Jake!" Amanda gives me a big hug. "What about your racing car?" she asks.

"I'll still get it," I tell her. "It'll just take a little longer."

"That's so sweet," she says. "I know you've been working really hard to save."

She hugs me, and I feel like I made the right choice. "It'll go by fast," I gulp.

Time flies when you're having fun, I think. At least I really hope so.

Chapter 10

The best things in life are free

It's the Friday night before the Christmas holidays. The year 4s have just finished their performance. We had to wait in our classroom while they sang. Now we come in through the backstage side door, so the audience can't see us.

I've got my toga on over my gym shorts. The knot is tied tightly. Both sides are closed with as many safety pins as Mum and Amanda could fit. I'm wearing my gold belt and sandals.

Nellie, Estella, Brittany and Ashley are wearing make-up. Their cheeks are rosy, their lips are glossy, and their hair is shiny.

We have silly laurel wreaths around our heads. Actually, the girls' wreaths look pretty.

My hands are sweaty. My stomach feels jumpy. I couldn't eat my dinner. I'm not sure I remember any of my lines. My glasses keep sliding down the bridge of my nose and I have to push them back up. I never noticed how much I do this until Adam videotaped us practising.

Nellie is jiggling her arms and switching her weight from one leg to the other.

"Take a deep breath," Estella tells us both.

Nellie and I breathe in and out.

"I think I'm going to be sick," says Nellie.

Me, too, I want to say. But I don't want to say that in front of Brittany.

Brittany shakes out her arms and then her legs. "I'm feeling nervous, too."

Now I'm worried about Brittany. I don't want her to feel nervous. "You look nice," I tell her.

She smiles and says, "You too. Like Hercules Jones."

"Really?" I say, amazed. Hercules Jones is this awesome character in a series of books that we've all read. He has dyslexia, like Adam. He finds out his ancestors are Greek gods. He has superpowers. He's cool. Brittany thinks I look like him? I try not to blush.

Ms Anderson is waving her cue cards on the other side of the stage. Adam makes the lights backstage blink on and off. That means it's time to start.

The lights in the hall go dim, and the lights onstage go bright. The kids take their places. Ms Anderson motions for Nellie to start.

I hear Nellie give her introduction. It sounds perfect. The audience gives her a big round of applause.

Then the curtain goes slowly, painfully, up.

I'm supposed to walk out. My legs don't want to do it.

Walk, legs. You're King Midas. You can do it.

I take a deep breath. I walk onstage. I look out at a gazillion faces. The lights are shining right in my eyes.

The hall is dark. The audience is huge. Where is my family?

I take a deep breath. Out of the corner of my eye, I see Ms Anderson holding up my cue card. I'm supposed to start. Now.

I take one more breath. Adam is standing next to Ms Anderson. He smiles and does a Worry Warrior hand signal.

I can do this. I'm like Hercules Jones. I think about all the millions of times we practised our lines. And Adam videotaped us. I think about how Mum helped me learn my song, and Amanda helped me with my costume.

I scoop up a handful of gold pieces and look right out at the audience. "Gold, gold, gold," I say. My voice is loud and clear. I'm projecting. "How I love gold."

Estella dances out with Ashley and Brittany. We all remember our lines. I don't drop anything, or fall off the stage, or knock anything over.

I think I might have done all right. I really hope so.

After my eyes adjust, I find Mum and Amanda in the audience. They've brought Mrs Jensen, too.

I'm having fun! The audience watches intently. They laugh at the funny parts, and they look worried at the sad parts.

When we reach the end, we all stand together and sing "The Best Things in Life Are Free." The crowd goes wild. We get a standing ovation. It's the best school play ever.

ABOUT THE AUTHOR

Marne Ventura is the author of 29 children's books, 10 of them for Capstone. A former primary school teacher, she holds a master's degree in education from the University of California. When she's not writing, she enjoys arts and crafts, cooking and baking, and spending time with her family. Marne lives with her husband on the central coast of California. This is her first venture into fiction.

ABOUT THE ILLUSTRATOR

Leo Trinidad is an illustrator and animator who has created many animated characters and television shows for companies including Disney and Dreamworks, but his great passion is illustrating children's books. Leo graduated with honours from the Veritas University of Arts and Design in San Jose, Costa Rica, where he lives with his wife and daughter. Visit him online at www.leotrinidad.com

GLOSSARY

astrophysicist scientist who studies objects in space such as planets, stars and moons

clove spice used in cooking

dyslexia learning disability that is usually marked by problems in reading, spelling and writing

electronics products that run on small amounts of electricity, including laptops, smart phones and TVs

eucalyptus fragrant evergreen tree

mythology old or ancient stories told again and again that help connect people with the past

narrator person who tells a story or describes an event

programmer person who writes instructions to make a computer work a certain way

project make your voice carry very far

satyr creature in Greek mythology with a face and body like a human and ears, legs, and tail like a goat

videotape record both the picture and sound

Viking group of Scandinavian warriors who raided other Europen countries in the 8th to 10th centuries

TALK ABOUT IT

1. Jake was really nervous about having such a big part in the school play, so he talked to his friends about his worries. What else might he have done?

2. Jake admits that he misses his sister now that she is at secondary school. Talk about how you've felt when a sibling or friend moved away.

3. Jake really wanted a robot car more than anything in the world. Has there ever been anything you've wanted that much? What did you do to try to get it?

WRITE ABOUT IT

1. Think about a time you were worried about something. Write about how you felt and what you did to feel better.

2. Who is your favourite character in this story? Draw a picture of that person. Then write a list of five things you like about him or her.

3. How would you have helped Jake with his worry? Think about that, and then write down what you would have done.

READ THEM ALL!

Worry WARRIORS

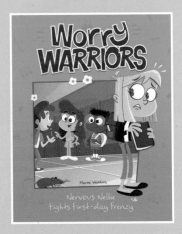

Nervous Nellie
Fights First-day Frenzy

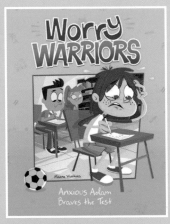

Anxious Adam
Braves the Test

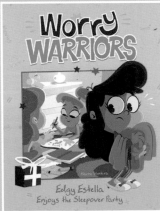

Edgy Estella
Enjoys the Sleepover Party

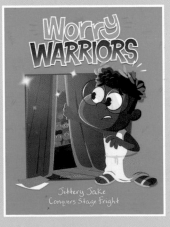

Jittery Jake
Conquers Stage Fright